THIS MAGI BOOK BELONGS TO:

_____

_____

_____

_____

*For Jamie*
~J.S.
*For Toby and Charlie*
~T.W.

*Reprinted 1998 (Twice)*

This paperback edition published 1997

First published in 1997 by Magi Publications
22 Manchester Street, London W1M 5PG

Text © 1997 Julie Sykes
Illustrations © 1997 Tim Warnes

Julie Sykes and Tim Warnes have asserted their rights
to be identified as the author and illustrator of this work
under the Copyright, Designs and Patents Act, 1988.

Printed and bound in Belgium by Proost NV, Turnhout

ISBN 1 85430 421 6

# I don't want to have a bath!

*by* Julie Sykes

*illustrated by* Tim Warnes

Little Tiger was very lively.
He liked to play exciting games.
He didn't mean to get dirty,
but somehow he always did.
Then Mummy Tiger would say,
"Little Tiger, you need a bath."
And each time Little Tiger
would answer,
"I don't *want* to have a bath!"

When Mummy Tiger took Little Tiger
down to the river one day to clean
him up, he wouldn't get into the water.
"Bathing is fun," said Mummy Tiger,
but Little Tiger didn't think so.
"I don't want to have a bath!" he cried
and he hurried off into the jungle
before she could make him.

First Little Tiger played with his
good friend, Little Monkey.
They climbed up trees
and swung from vines.
Little Tiger fell off
and dirtied his paws.

Then Mummy Monkey
shouted, "Bath time,
Little Monkey and Little
Tiger, too!"
"I don't want to have a
bath!" cried Little Tiger
and with a flash of his
dirty paws he scurried
past Mummy Monkey
and into the bushes.

Next Little Tiger went to play with his old friend, Little Bear. They wriggled into bushes and searched for ripe berries. Little Tiger got berry juice all over his face.

Then Daddy Bear growled, "Bath time,
Little Bear and Little Tiger, too!"
"I don't want to have a bath!" said Little Tiger
and twitching his berry stained whiskers he
scampered past Daddy
Bear and down to the
water hole.

Down at the water hole Little Tiger met his dear friend, Little Elephant. They started to play fight and Little Elephant squirted mud all over Little Tiger's coat.

Then Daddy Elephant trumpeted, "Bath time, Little Elephant and Little Tiger, too!"
"I don't want to have a bath!" answered Little Tiger and shaking his muddy paws he raced past Daddy Elephant and out on to the grassy plain.

Little Tiger called on his new friend, Little Rhino next. They charged around in the grass and Little Tiger got grass seeds in his tail. Then Mummy Rhino roared, "Bath time, Little Rhino and Little Tiger, too!"

"I don't want to have a bath!" said Little Tiger and swishing his grassy tail he galloped past Mummy Rhino and back into the jungle.

Little Tiger wondered
who to play with next. The jungle
seemed very quiet and nothing moved,
not even an ant!
Sadly, Little Tiger began to wander home.
But wait – what was that?

Little Tiger looked up
and saw. . .

. . . a handsome peacock, showing
off his tail.

"How beautiful," gasped Little Tiger.
"Will you come and play with me?"

The peacock turned up his beak. "Play with *you*?" he said. "No thanks!" "Why not?" asked Little Tiger in surprise. "Because you're too dirty," said the peacock scornfully. "You would spoil my lovely feathers. You need a bath," he added, and tossing his head off he strutted.

"Stupid peacock!" said Little Tiger, feeling hurt. "Of course I don't need a bath."

Little Tiger wandered on until he reached the river. Playing with his friends had made him thirsty and he stopped to have a drink. "Who's *that*?" he cried, seeing a reflection in the water. "It can't be me. I'm not *that* dirty."

He leaned over to look more carefully –
and he toppled right in!

Little Tiger spluttered to the surface.
"It *was* me," he cried. "What a mess I looked!"
Quickly Little Tiger began to bath. He splished
and splashed in the warm water. It was fun,
just as Mummy Tiger said it would be.
Once he was clean, Little Tiger climbed back
on to the bank to admire his reflection.
Wouldn't Mummy Tiger be pleased!

Just then, Little Leopard tumbled by.
"Hello, Little Tiger," he called. "Will you play
with me?" Little Tiger looked at Little
Leopard's grubby fur and shook his head.
"No thanks," he said. "You're *much* too
dirty to play with me. You would
spoil my nice clean coat.
You need a bath!"

And puffing out his silky chest
Little Tiger hurried home.

Some more books from
**Magi Publications**
for you to enjoy.

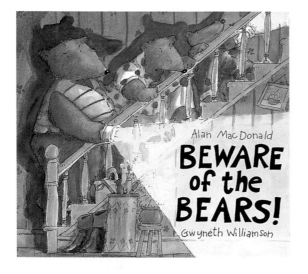

Alan MacDonald
**BEWARE of the BEARS!**
Gwyneth Williamson

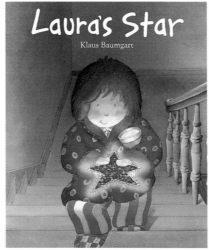

Laura's Star
Klaus Baumgart

I don't want to go to bed!
Julie Sykes
Tim Warnes

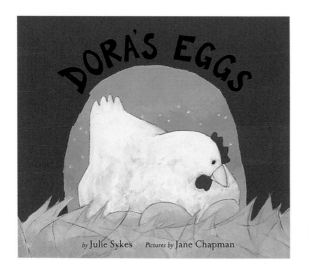

DORA'S EGGS
by Julie Sykes   Pictures by Jane Chapman

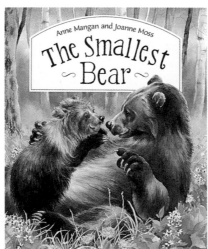

Anne Mangan and Joanne Moss
The Smallest Bear

Hurry, Santa!
Julie Sykes
Tim Warnes

All books available from most booksellers. In case of difficulty please contact
Magi Publications, 22 Manchester Street, London W1M 5PG, UK